BOOK ONE

OTHER BOOKS BY ADAM REX

DIGESTION! THE MUSICAL, ILLUSTRATED BY LAURA PARK

★ "This showstopper gives the purposes and processes of digestion the lavish, glitzy production they deserve, from teeth to toilet. . . . [C]ertain to receive thunderous ovations."
—*Kirkus Reviews*, starred review

ON ACCOUNT OF THE GUM

★ "Rex is king of the picture books. Consider this required reading."
—*Booklist*, starred review

★ "[G]loriously giggly."

—*Kirkus Reviews*, starred review

★ "Progressively, hilariously, outrageous."
—*Horn Book Magazine*, starred review

UNSTOPPABLE, ILLUSTRATED BY LAURA PARK

★ "[N]ot only funny . . . and beautiful to look at . . . it also hints at collaboration's role in effecting change."
—*Publishers Weekly*, starred review

★ "[Features] the page turn of the year. . . . Ridiculously fun."
—*Booklist*, starred review

WHY?, ILLUSTRATED BY CLAIRE KEANE

★ "[A] story-time home run—hilarious, heartfelt, instructive, and interactive."

—*Booklist*, starred review

NOTHING RHYMES WITH ORANGE

★ "A sly concept, deft artwork, and unflagging energy make this a winner."

—*Publishers Weekly*, starred review

★ "A perfect read-aloud. Fruitful in every sense of the word."
—*Kirkus Reviews*, starred review

THE STORY OF GUMLUCK THE WIZARD

BOOK ONE

ADAM REX

chronicle books · san francisco

Library of Congress Cataloging-in-Publication Data available.

ISBN 978-1-7972-1323-1

Manufactured in China.

Design by Aya Ghanameh.
Typeset in Domaine and Balster.

10 9 8 7 6 5 4 3 2 1

Chronicle Books LLC
680 Second Street
San Francisco, California 94107

Chronicle Books—we see things differently.
Become part of our community at www.chroniclekids.com.

For Lauren Pettapiece, whom I've never met. But she draws these raccoons, and her raccoon drawings make me feel a certain way, and in trying to capture that feeling I eventually wrote this, a book with no raccoons. That's how it works sometimes. So if you've ever wanted to ask an author where they get their ideas, now you know: raccoon drawings.

Gumluck's Guests

Let me tell you how I met the wizard Gumluck.

It was Monday.

"It is Monday!" he said, in his little brass bed, in the hill that he used for a house.

On Mondays Gumluck had visitors.

He changed out of his nightgown and into his daygown.

"So much to do!"

(Look at him, hopping around, ridiculous. What a buggy-bumper.)

He used magic to sweep the floors.

He made magic to polish the candelabra.

That's when he saw that his upstairs pumpkin was downstairs, and his downstairs pumpkin was upstairs.

If you are not a wizard, you probably don't have upstairs pumpkins and downstairs pumpkins. Or maybe you do, but you don't mind mixing them up. I think that is very smart of you.

"Such a mess," Gumluck sighed. "And everything must be just right for my guests."

So he pushed his pumpkins into place and walked outside to have a look at his house. A raven was in the yard, hunting for sticks and straw.

That's me. I am the raven. Maybe you didn't know you were reading a story told by a raven. If you do not like it, you can leave.

But look. This is a story about helping and haunting. A story of good lies and bad truths. Ghosts and gold. The story of a dance, a disaster, and the day I fell in love. So you might as well stay—because most of all I want to tell you that last part, and it doesn't happen until the end.

"Old Lady Crow," the wizard said to me, "today I will have visitors from town! They like to come say hello, you know how it is."

I fluffed my feathers and said, "Humph." I am not so old. And I am certainly not a crow.

"You know, the townspeople call me the Little Wizard Who Lives in the Big Hill!" Gumluck said.

Then he chewed his lip. "But do you think my hill is big enough?"

I do not know, I thought, *and I do not care*.

He said, "What if someone comes looking for the Little Wizard Who Lives in the Big Hill, and when they see my hill they say, '*That* is not so big! This must not be the place.' They might walk right by without stopping. That wouldn't do."

Gumluck the Wizard rolled up his sleeves and made a shovel out of magic. He made a bucket out of magic. He shoveled mud out of his shoveling hole, and bucketed mud to the hilltop, where he plopped it.

Then back down the hill to shovel some more,
and back to the top,

plop.

By his 44th fill, the top of the hill had grown so tall it touched the treetops. So tall that Gumluck's magic bucket bumped the hickory tree. The same tree where I had been building with sticks and straw.

And that's when my nest fell from its branch and was dashed to pieces on the ground.

I croaked. But—

Shovel and plop,
he did not stop. He didn't know what he had done. He shoveled and plopped from the hole to the top until he thought he had shoveled enough.

"Now *that* is a big hill, Old Lady Crow!" he told me. "Wouldn't you say?"

"Farfle!" is what I said.

I shouldn't have—I was angry. Don't you go saying *farfle*. It is a grown-up word, for when bumpkins with pumpkins knock nests out of hickory trees.

"Oh!" said Gumluck. "Listen!" So though I was mad I did listen, to the sound of footsteps coming through the forest. "Someone is coming!" he cheered.

Gumluck raced back inside his home in the hill. He owed me a nest, so I raced right after him.

The little wizard took off his hat and measured himself against the wall. "I know what you are thinking, Old Lady Crow," he told me. "You are thinking, 'The hill is big enough, but is that wizard little enough?'"

(This is not what I was thinking.)

Gumluck said, "What if I open my door to visitors and they say, 'We were looking for the *Little* Wizard Who Lives in the Big Hill, but *you* are not so little! This must not be the place! Goodbye!' That would not do at all."

(I could tell you what I was thinking, but I am not allowed to put those words in a book.)

"Every week I measure myself from the bottom of my feet to the top of my hair," said Gumluck.

"And every week I find I have grown, just a bit. So now I have to magic myself back down to size."

I flapped my wings and said,

I said,

I told him.

I finished.

Like I told you—I was mad about my nest.

Gumluck tilted his chin.

"I think I had better shrink myself a little," he said. "Just in case."

And then Gumluck used magic to make his legs shorter.

"Now I am ready for visitors!"

I wonder—are you all like this? I haven't lived near humans much. You take some getting used to.

"Look, about my nest," I said, just as there was a knock at the door.

Gumluck's first visitor was a woman from town.

"Hello, hello!" said Gumluck as he let her in. "Did you notice how big my hill is? And how little I am? Just how you townspeople like it, right?" Gumluck picked at his sleeves. "Right?"

The woman didn't care to talk about hills and wizards. The woman did not even say hello. She needed a dress for the Harvest Dance, and she seemed to think it was Gumluck's job to make her one.

"Ah, the Harvest Dance!" sighed the little wizard. "Music and dancing under the stars." He leaned toward the woman with a sly look. "And every year the townspeople crown a Harvest Hero. I wonder who you will choose to be Harvest Hero *this* year."

"I don't know," said the woman. "So . . . the dress?"

"Oh, sure."

Gumluck used magic to teach some mice and birds how to sew, and he sent them all away together.

"Great," the woman said.

She made a face as she left.

I watched this from the windowsill. "I think she just wanted you to make her a dress," I said.

"But now she will get her dress *and* a wonderful story," said the wizard.

"Hmph."

His second visitor was a man who wanted muscles.

He did not say hello, either. I guess no one says hello in this kingdom.

"Muscles, eh?" said Gumluck. "Muscles to show off at the Harvest Dance, I suppose! Maybe you are hoping to be crowned Harvest Hero? It is not about muscles, though. The king says the Harvest Hero should be the person who has done the most to help the town."

"I just want muscles," said the man. "And I don't want to exercise."

Gumluck nodded like he understood. He snapped his fingers. And then the man had a lot of muscles.

Too, too, too many muscles.

"You should see what he did to my *nest*," I told the man as he muscled angrily out the door.

"Was he frowning?" asked Gumluck. "Or did his new face muscles make it look like he was frowning?"

"Maybe he was frowning about his new face muscles," I said.

The third visitor was a prince. From the castle, I guess. I never learned his name, so I am going to call him Prince Whoop-de-doo.

He rode up—*whoosh*—in a shiny carriage with horses. It was all very pretty. Very, very pretty. You know how some things are so pretty they're ugly? It was like that.

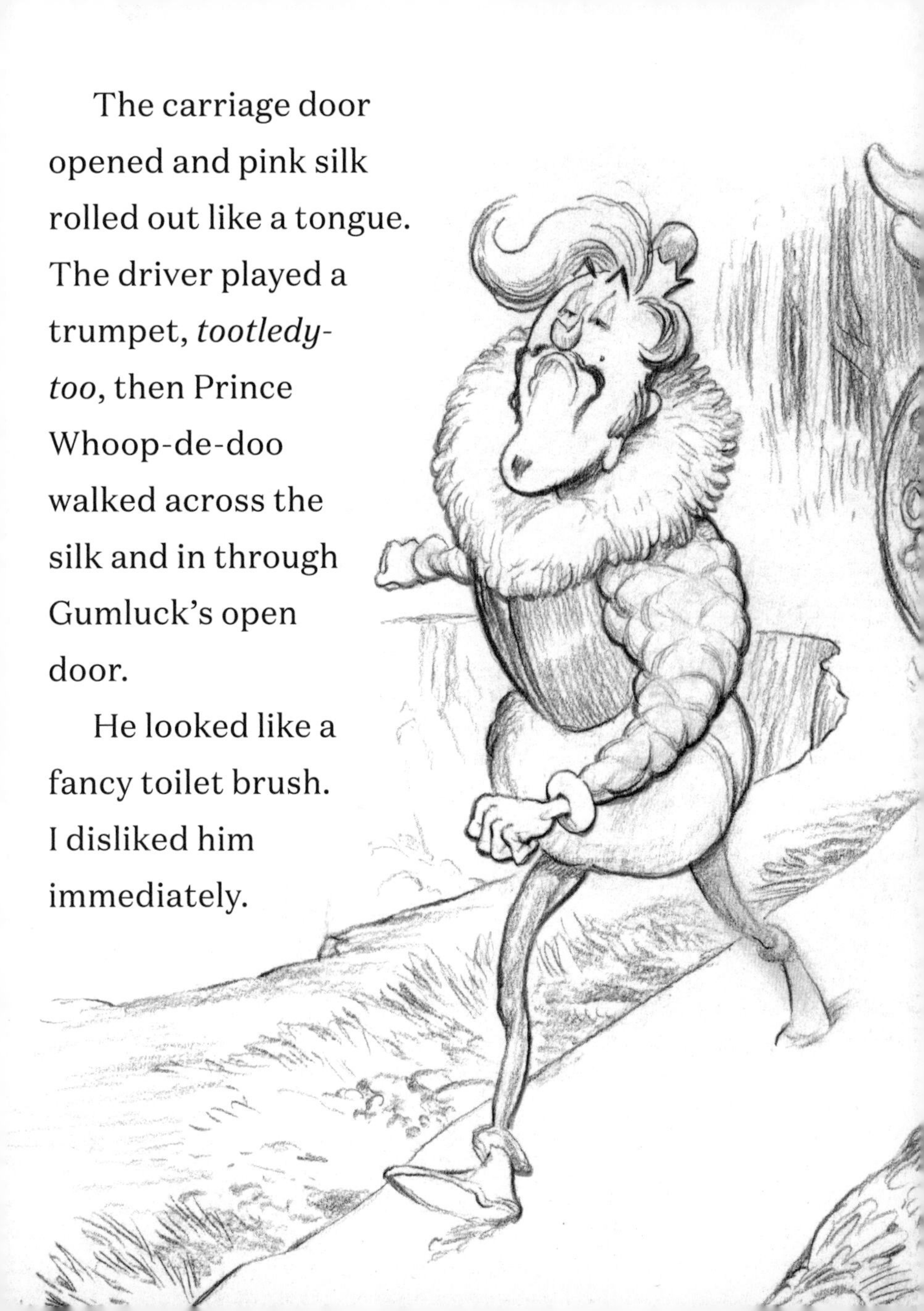

The carriage door opened and pink silk rolled out like a tongue. The driver played a trumpet, *tootledy-too*, then Prince Whoop-de-doo walked across the silk and in through Gumluck's open door.

He looked like a fancy toilet brush. I disliked him immediately.

He said, "Wizard, I *order* you to make Lady Pamplemousse fall in *love* with me."

"Oh," said Gumluck.

"I *tried* ordering Lady *Pamplemousse*," the prince explained, "but it did not *work*."

Gumluck squirmed. "I . . . could do that," he said. "Why does my tummy hurt?"

"Because it is wrong," I said. "Even a noodle-head knows that. Love cannot be taken—love is a gift. It has to be given."

Prince Whoop-de-doo scowled at Gumluck and said, "Then you *have* to make her *give* her love to *me*."

I said, "You do not have to do that."

The prince pouted. "Look, are you going to do it or *not*?"

Gumluck looked like he might faint.

"I . . . am not," he said. I could see it was hard work for him, saying it. So he quickly made the man a lollipop out of magic and held the door for him.

“Sorry!” he added. “So sorry. Good luck with that lady!”

The prince grumbled as he left. “Silly wizard. Probably would have turned me into a *toad* by *mistake*.”

I spat. “You were a toad when you got here!”

Then the prince went back in his carriage, *tootledy-too*, the silk rolled up, and *whoosh*.

We were alone. "Too bad," Gumluck said. He picked at the star on his robe. "I guess that prince will tell his friends at the Harvest Dance that I wasn't helpful at all."

I wanted to tell him that terrible toads do not have any friends, but sadly, that isn't true. Rich princes with full pockets will always have many friends, standing near, waiting for the money to fall out.

Besides, I had not forgotten about my nest. I said, "Listen, butternut, if you help *anyone* today, it should be—"

I was interrupted by a fourth visitor.

A man with tears on his face. Great.

"My daughter!" he cried. "She's lost in the Haunted Forest!"

Without a word, Gumluck leaped up and ran out the door.

"What?" I squawked. I took wing and chased after him. "What are you doing?" I called.

He didn't answer.

"Are you running into the Haunted Forest? Fool. You are too foolish to know what is good for you," I said. "Stop and think. It is a dangerous place; many of the ghosts there are hungry and hateful."

"Yes," said Gumluck as he ran. "It is no place for a child."

It was easy to see where the regular forest ended and the Haunted Forest began. It was like a black eye on a pretty face. Gumluck ran in through the rotten trees and the sobbing rain.

I stopped at the edge of it, afraid.

I could not see Gumluck anymore. "Silly," I said. "Silly wizard. You don't just run into the Haunted Forest."

I know all about the Haunted Forest.

The wind howled through rickety branches.

I said, “All right! Enough’s enough. Come back now.”

Lightning flashed and thunder crashed.

I sniffed. He was gone. *That's too bad*, I thought. Plus he owed me a nest.

Then, to my surprise, Gumluck walked back through thick shadows with a girl in his arms.

Back at the house in the hill, the father hugged his daughter tight and rushed her back to town.

"There they go, Old Lady Crow," said Gumluck. "Home to a warm bath and a warm bed."

I sat on the mailbox and clucked.

"Unbelievable. You clean. You shovel. You shrink yourself to please them. You do what they ask. You do not complain. You do not even make them say thank you!"

Gumluck dangled his little legs over the edge of the big hole. "A thank-you is a gift," he said. "It has to be given."

"Well, yes," I said. "Even a noodlehead knows that." I ruffled my feathers. "Still, some people want too much and give too little."

Gumluck nodded and looked at his toes. "I want something," he admitted. "But it is a secret."

"Hmm," I said. "Is your secret that you want to be crowned Harvest Hero at the Harvest Dance?"

He shivered. “How did you know that? Are you a wizard, too, Old Lady Crow?”

He could have used a warm bath himself—he was cold and wet from the rain. I wondered just what he’d seen in that Haunted Forest.

I decided I could complain about my nest later.

“Please stop calling me Old Lady Crow,” I said. “I am a raven, and my name is Helvetica.”

It is, you know. Helvetica is my name. How do you do?

The wizard smiled. “And I am Gumluck!” he said. “The people in town call me the Little Wizard Who Lives in the Big Hill.”

Actually, now the people in town were calling him the Shrinking Wizard Who Lives Next to a Big Hole, but I didn’t know that yet.

GUMLUCK

Gumluck's Ghost

On Tuesday, Gumluck felt funny.

"*Helvetica!*" he called out the window. "I feel funny!"

"You feel funny," I said—but quietly, so Gumluck would not hear. "A fish feels finny." I was working on my new nest. "A fake feels phony. Everything feels like something."

"*Helvetica?*"

Not my problem, I thought. *This nest is my problem.*

But then I had a memory of Gumluck, running through the wicked trees. That little girl had not been his problem, either.

“Guh,” I sighed. I brought Gumluck a wet washcloth and took his temperature.

“Hemmo, Hewfediga!” he said with the thermometer in his mouth. “I feew fuddy.”

“Hush. Lie still.”

He lay still. I checked the thermometer.

“You are haunted,” I said.

“I am what?” asked Gumluck.

“I told you not to go in that forest.” I showed Gumluck the mirror. There was a ghost in his hair.

"Just a little one," I said. "And it does not look angry. You got lucky."

The ghost was humming to himself.

"I can't have a ghost in my hair," Gumluck whispered, so as not to insult the ghost. "The Harvest Dance is this Sunday." He looked glum. "Whoever heard of a Harvest Hero with a ghost in their hair?"

"Get some fresh air," I suggested. "Maybe it will fly away."

"Will you come with—"

"No."

So Gumluck and the ghost took a walk.

Thanks to the bird network, I know everything they said and did. Remember that, kids: Birds are always watching you, and we tell each other *everything*.

"Are you still there?" Gumluck asked the ghost.

"I keep hearing a voice," said the ghost. "Maybe this big old house is already haunted."

"Are you talking about me?" asked Gumluck.

"There it is again," said the ghost.

"I am not big," said Gumluck. "Or old. Or a house."

The ghost floated down to look at him. "You have two windows like a house."

"Windows?"

"And a door."

"I don't think I do."

"You have gabled dormers."

"I don't know what that is, but no."

"Do we have to keep walking around," asked the ghost, "or can we get ice cream?"

So they got ice cream.

"Well, here we are," said Gumluck as ice cream dripped down his fingers. He had walked them right up to the edge of the Haunted Forest.

"Yes . . . here we are," said the ghost. "And . . . why are we here?"

"I thought you might want to go home," said Gumluck. "Home to the Haunted Forest. And not be in my hair anymore."

The ghost hid under Gumluck's hat. "No, thank you," he said.

Inside the Haunted Forest, it was darkly windy. Skeleton trees clawed at the windy dark.

"Are you afraid?" Gumluck asked the ghost.

The ghost's voice sounded small. "There are ghosts that even other ghosts are scared of."

“Which kind of ghost are you?”

“Well, ghosts are *supposed* to be scary, but no one has ever been scared of me. And if I must be a ghost, I want to be good at it. So I’ve decided to practice by haunting a little house of my own.”

"I am not a house," said Gumluck. "I am sorry, but I think you will have to find somewhere else to live."

"I do not live anywhere," said the ghost. "Because ghosts are dead."

"Then I think you will have to find somewhere else to be dead," said Gumluck. "The Harvest Dance is this Sunday."

"Good," said the ghost. "We will go to the dance together. Not like a date, though—just as friends."

Gumluck thought. "People call me the Little Wizard Who Lives in the Big Hill," he said. "If you stay in my hair, they might start calling me the Haunted Wizard . . . or . . . or Ghost Head."

He smiled a bit, thinking about it. Those were pretty good names, actually.

Gumluck walked back to the hill with the ghost in his hair. "Tell me about your death," he said, "and I will tell you about my life."

"You first," said the ghost, who wanted time to think.

"Ah. My life is a very interesting subject," said the wizard. "I was born a baby."

"Explain," said the ghost.

"Imagine me," said Gumluck, "but with a head that is too big and legs that are too small."

"You *have* a head that is too big," said the ghost. "You *have* legs that are too small. You have that now."

"Yes," agreed Gumluck. "I used to be very old. But I didn't like it much, so I decided to be very young."

He stopped walking a moment and thought. It was hard doing both at the same time.

"I think I used to have a big brain, but fewer feelings. And now I have big feelings . . . but maybe not so many brains?"

He began moving again, and his face brightened.

"And then some other things happened, and then I met you! And that is my life."

"*Amazing,*" said the ghost.

"Now it is your turn," said the wizard. "Were you always a ghost?"

"No," said the ghost. "Once I was a mighty warrior. Tall, with big muscles and a mustache. I was *very* scary and brave, and I had many adventures."

"What was your name?"

"Butterscotch."

From my perch in the hickory tree I could see the two of them, wizard and ghost, coming home. I was building my new nest lower than before. If you had asked me why, I do not think I would have known the answer. I guess I thought it would be nice on that stout branch, close to the ground. It was just by chance that it was right next to Gumluck's kitchen window.

When they came up to the hill, the ghost said, "So you're a house, but you live inside a bigger house? Weird."

"I am not a house," said Gumluck.

"Still haunted?" I asked him.

"Oh!" said Gumluck. "Dear Butterscotch, just look. Poor Helvetica is stuck in a tree."

I frowned and said, "I am not stuck."

"Is Helvetica a treehouse?" asked Butterscotch.

"I am a raven," I told him. "I am supposed to sit in trees."

"She says she's supposed to sit in trees," said the ghost.

Gumluck was winking at me. Wink wink wink. I didn't care for it.

He said, "I have never seen her sit in a tree."

"I know *that's* true," I muttered. If he had seen me in a tree, he would have seen my nest. I wouldn't be rebuilding it in the first place.

Wink wink wink. "She is stuck way up high," said Gumluck, "and needs a brave, scary ghost to frighten her down."

Butterscotch shrugged, sort of. He didn't really have shoulders. "Maybe I am not scary enough."

"You are, without a doubt, the scariest ghost here," said Gumluck.

That puffed the ghost up a little.

"Hel-VE-ti-ca!" Gumluck called. "Can you HEAR ME?"

"You are only ten feet away," I said.

"DO YOU NEED BUTTERSCOTCH TO SAVE YOU?"

I figured Gumluck wanted me to play along. I rolled my eyes.

"You are both ridiculous," I sniffed. But then I was smiling before I knew what was happening. "Fine. Save me."

"Poor little house," said Butterscotch, and he floated up to the branch beside me. "OK. I will scare her down."

"BOO," said Butterscotch.

"Boo yourself," I answered.

"BOOWOOWOOOOO."

"Oh my goodness, look, a ghost," I said.

"This tree is haunted," the ghost told me. "Spoooooky tree. So get down, little raven. BOOWOOWOOWOOOOO!"

Butterscotch turned in wobbly circles, and he wasn't being too careful about it. I saw what was going to happen a moment before it did—and a moment too late to stop it.

"BOOOOOOOOOOOOOOOOOOOO
OOOOOOOOOOOOOOOOOOOOOO
OOOOOOOOOOOOOOO
OOOOOO

OOOOOOOOOO
OOOOOOOOOOOOOOOOOO
OOOOOOOOOOOOOO!" said the ghost.

"Oh, look out!" I cried.

Butterscotch plowed right through my new nest. The sticks and straw of it flew apart and fell, rattling, to the ground.

He did not even know what he had done. No one notices a nest.

"Keep it up!" cheered Gumluck. "Helvetica is starting to look scared! Or angry or sad or something."

Well. I wasn't as angry or sad as you might think. That nest was turning out cockeyed anyway.

I sighed and hopped onto the mailbox. "My hero," I said.

"It worked! Hooray!" said Gumluck. "Thank goodness Helvetica is safe. What a brave ghost." Wink wink.

Butterscotch snuggled back into Gumluck's hair, looking very proud.

"I'll tell you what," said the wizard to the ghost. "I will vote for you for Harvest Hero, and you can vote for me."

"Then I can stay?"

"I guess maybe you can," said the wizard. "We make a nice team."

"You know what rhymes with nice team?" asked the ghost.

So we all got some ice cream.

Gumluck and the Good Lie

On Wednesdays, Gumluck the Wizard did his shopping at the market in town. I stayed home, next to Gumluck's hill.

Can you guess what I was doing?

Go on, guess.

I was building another new nest.

"Pick me up some cranberries," I told Gumluck as he left his house in the hill. He had a bag in his hands and a bag on his head.

"Why am I wearing a bag?" Gumluck asked the ghost who haunted his hair.

"So the townspeople will not see me," said Butterscotch. "I am pretty scary."

"That's true," Gumluck remembered with a smile. "You scared Helvetica right out of the hickory tree."

He did *not*. He did not *scare* me out of the hickory tree. It is important to me that you know this.

In the market square, Gumluck shopped for cranberries and rutabagas. The farmer told him about someone called the Shrinking Wizard Who Lives Next to a Big Hole.

Did you catch that?

The people in town call *Gumluck* the Shrinking Wizard Who Lives Next to a Big Hole, but he doesn't know it. He thinks they call him the Little Wizard Who Lives in the Big Hill, so he thought the farmer was talking about someone else. And the farmer did not recognize Gumluck, because the little wizard had a bag on his head.

It was a big mix-up. A *bag* mix-up. I could have straightened it all out, if I had been there. And I might have been there, except SOMEONE KEEPS WRECKING MY NEST.

So Gumluck said, "I thought I knew all the wizards! But I have never heard of the Shrinking Wizard Who Lives Next to a Big Hole."

"He is a *joke*," said the farmer. "They say he talks to his hair."

"Sounds like a funny fellow," said Gumluck.

Next he went shopping for ice cream and bacon. The butcher told him the Shrinking Wizard Who Lives Next to a Big Hole knew only silly things—not useful things. Myths but no maths. Spells but not spelling.

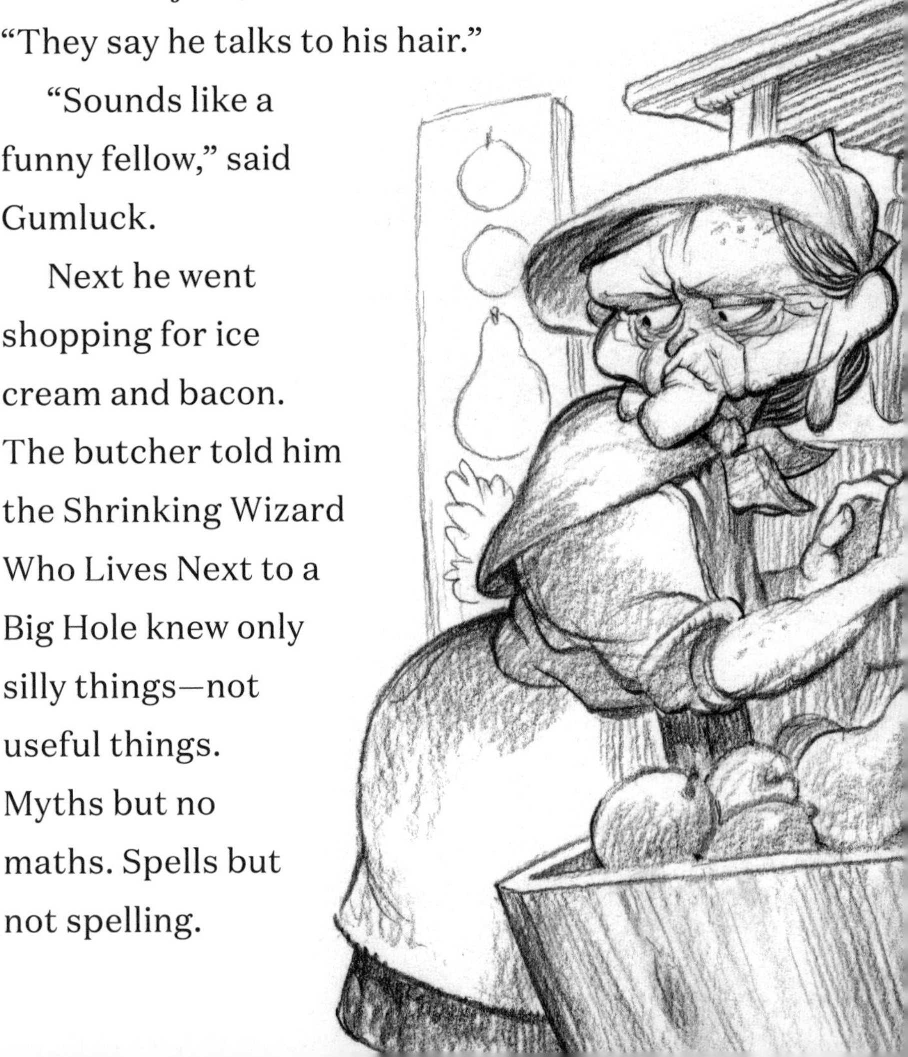

"I'll bet he can't even spell *spell,*" said the butcher.

"It takes all kinds of people to make a world," Gumluck reckoned.

"Why do you have a bag on your head?" asked the butcher.

Gumluck said, "I think I hear someone calling my name. Goodbye!" And he jogged away.

"Thank you for not telling about me," said Butterscotch. "That was a good lie."

Gumluck said later it made his face feel hot. He was not sure the words *good* and *lie* should go together.

Gumluck bought marmalade from the marmalady and bread from the baker.

"Say," said Gumluck to the baker. "I wonder who might be crowned the Harvest Hero this Sunday. Has anyone in the kingdom been—I don't know—*extra* helpful this year?"

The baker said, "Anyone but that Shrinking Wizard—what a clown! He does whatever we tell him, but he always screws it up."

"Don't you townspeople talk about anything else?" asked the ghost.

The baker frowned at the bag. "Was that your voice? It sounded strange."

Gumluck cleared his throat. "I said, 'Why does he do what you tell him?'" he said. "This Shrinking Wizard, I mean."

The baker shrugged. "He wants so badly for us to like him."

This made Gumluck sad. "It sounds like he needs a friend."

That awful Prince Whoop-de-doo was standing near, eating a cinnamon bun.

"Are you *talking* about the Shrinking *Wizard?*" said the prince with his mouth full. He spat specks of cinnamon bun when he spoke. I know because there was a mockingbird watching the prince, and she mocked him pretty hard about it when we played dominoes the next morning.

"That Shrinking Wizard did *not* do what *I* told him," whined Prince Whoop-de-doo. "And *everyone* is supposed to give me what I *want*. Take this cinnamon bun: I took this cinnamon bun! And I am *not* going to *pay* for it."

The baker looked at his feet. "Of course, Your Highness," he said.

"I have told *everyone* else in the market how *un*helpful that wizard is," the prince said to Gumluck. "And now I have told *you*." Then he walked away, licking his fingers.

Gumluck gathered up his things and told the baker goodbye. "Maybe you should vote for this Shrinking Wizard to be the Harvest Hero," Gumluck whispered to Butterscotch. "It might be the only vote he gets."

"I'll probably vote for myself," said the ghost.

On his way out of town, Gumluck shopped for candles and beeswax. He chose what he wanted and waited—waited for news of the famous Shrinking Wizard.

"Thirteen cents," said the candlestick maker.

"Oh," said Gumluck. He rummaged through his purse. "Here."

The man took the coins and nodded at Gumluck's tall stack of packages. "Last stop, I hope."

"Oh, yes," said Gumluck. "I am heading home to the forest."

"Oho, the forest!" answered the candlestick maker.

"Do you know who else makes his home in the forest? The Shrinking Wizard Who Lives Next to a Big Hole! That little fool doesn't even see how everyone laughs at him."

When they were alone, Gumluck uncovered his head. He and Butterscotch walked back to the hill.

"You live next to a big hole," said the ghost.

"Probably a lot of people do," Gumluck agreed.

When he got home, Gumluck came alone to talk with me at the hickory tree.

"Can a lie be good?" he wanted to know.

"Hmm. I think it can, if it only helps and doesn't hurt," I said. "The truth can hurt, too, you know."

"We lied to Butterscotch," he said. "We helped him think he was scary. I hope that was good. I would help that Shrinking Wizard, too, if I could."

“Shrinking Wizard? Who is that?” I asked, because I did not know.

So Gumluck told me all the funny stories he had heard about the Shrinking Wizard Who Lives Next to a Big Hole. All the stories about what a character he was. I listened.

When I had heard enough, I flew into town and dropped bird droppings on the heads of all the people in the market.

Gumluck and the Gold

On Thursday the king invited all the wizards in the kingdom to his castle for snacks. So Gumluck and I walked through the forest,

past the market,

beyond the neighborhood of houses,

and finally to the toe of a thin mountain. The castle was on top.

Gumluck had always admired the king's mountain. It was much, *much* taller than the wizard's hill.

"Why does the king invite you wizards for snacks?" I asked.

"Just to say hello," said Gumluck. "You know how it is."

"That is what you said about the townspeople," I reminded him. "And they all wanted favors, and not one of them said hello."

Gumluck thought. "*That* can't be right," he murmured.

Gumluck made himself some wings out of magic, and together we flew to the castle entrance. The mountain rumbled beneath us.

"Did the mountain just rumble?" I asked.

"It is probably hungry for snacks," said Gumluck.

We went in the castle door and through the Hall of Harvest Heroes. Paintings of past Heroes peered down at us from frames on the walls.

"That is Borgen Baffleton," said Gumluck, pointing to the first frame in the hall. "He was *very* helpful. A hundred years ago I made him a Potion of Smartness, and then he invented the

HALL of HARVEST HEROES
HARVEST HERO

word *and*! It made talking easier."

We walked on a bit, and Gumluck pointed at a painting of a woman wearing a wimple.

"That is Prudence Snakewrestler. She wrestled a snake!"

"A snake?"

"A *giant* snake!"

"All by herself?" I asked.

"All by herself," said Gumluck. "Well . . . I did cast a spell that made her better at wrestling. But she really helped the town—that snake was eating too many chickens."

"It sounds like you helped, too."

Gumluck blushed. "Except I was the one who

made the snake giant in the first place," he explained.

Farther on was a painting of a baby.

"A *baby*?!" I squawked. "Whatever could a baby have done that was so helpful to the town?"

"I never heard," said Gumluck. "But the king promised it had been very, very helpful."

The next painting was the same baby, but a year older. And then a year older than that. And a year older than that. In painting after painting, you could see the kid get older and older until I finally realized who it was.

"Wait, is this that snooty Prince Whoop-de-doo?"

"I do not think that is his name."

I huffed. "Prince Whoop-de-doo has been the Harvest Hero for the last . . . " I counted the paintings. "Twenty-five years? I don't believe it."

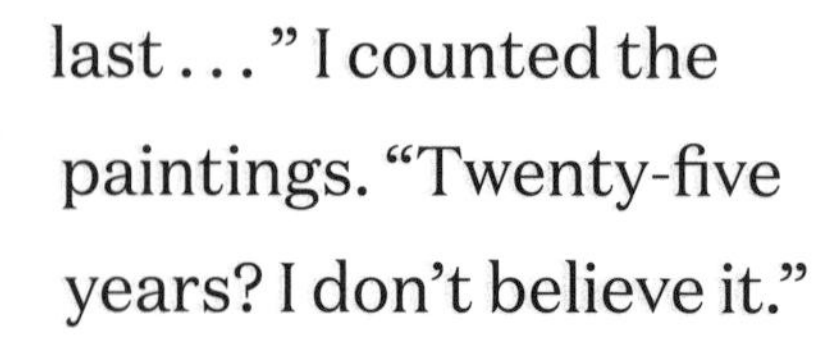

"The people must believe," said the wizard. "The people must believe in him very much, or they wouldn't keep voting for him."

"Hmm. And I bet his father, the king, counts the votes, doesn't he?"

"Yes! How did you guess?"

We met the king in his Treasure Room. The Treasure Room was filled with gold. And also ordinary things. Straw and sticks and a big stack of bricks.

Gumluck was hoping to see the Very Wise Wizard Who Lives in the Moon. He would have liked to see the Beautiful Wizard Who Carries His House in a Teapot, or the Round Wizard Who Tamed the Sky. He told me he especially wanted to meet the Shrinking Wizard Who Lives Next to a Big Hole.

"We sound like we have a lot in common," he said. And I said nothing, because I thought the truth might hurt his feelings. Is that a lie? Is it a good one?

Gumluck was the only wizard who came, anyway.

"I am the only wizard who *ever* comes," Gumluck whispered. "It must make the king very sad."

The king did not look very sad to me. "Do you know what would be funny?" he asked us. "If you turned all this straw into gold."

“I do not think that would be funny,” I said.

The king ignored me. “Try it and see,” he said. So Gumluck made magic and turned the straw into gold.

“I guess it was a little funny,” he said.

“Do you know what would be even funnier?” asked the king. “If you turned these *sticks* into gold.”

“I do not see why that would be any funnier,” I said.

“Only one way to find out,” said the king.

So Gumluck clapped his hands and the sticks turned into gold, solid gold.

The king grinned a big grin. “See? Do you see how funny it was?”

Gumluck shrugged.

I had been wondering why people kept going to Gumluck for favors if they thought he was such a screwup. Now I had my answer. Gumluck often got things a little bit wrong. But if, by chance, Gumluck did everything right, your greatest dreams could come true. And the little wizard never asked for a single thing in return. He must have seemed like a genie, full of wishes, with nothing to do but wait for his next command.

It bugged me. Birds don't treat people that way.

The king was having such a grand time that he couldn't stop laughing. He looked like he wanted to say something about the bricks.

"The king's snacks are usually pretty good," whispered Gumluck. "Cheese and crackers."

He leaned close.

"And they're free!"

Gumluck and the Bad Truth

"Farfle! No wonder the other wizards never come," I said the next day. "I think you should not visit that king anymore."

"What?" said Gumluck. "He's my friend."

"The king does not care about friends. The king cares about treasure."

Nearby, the little ghost hummed to himself as he messed around in the candelabra.

Gumluck had a thoughtful look. "I believe friends are the real treasure in life."

"And the king believes treasure is the real treasure in life," I told him, and blew a raspberry. "He's a crumb-bum."

Gumluck squirmed. "You have such interesting names for people."

And what if I do? Some people need help understanding all the things they do wrong. I help a lot of people that way.

"You need to make a change," I told Gumluck. "You help everyone in town with your magic. You are waiting for a thank-you, like a crown at the Harvest Dance. You want to be their Harvest Hero, so you keep helping and helping, because you think helping is what they like about you. But . . . you are good, Gumluck."

I suddenly felt embarrassed.

"You are . . . you should . . . you should have people who just *like* you," I said. "Even if you do not help them. Even if, by accident, you *hurt* them. By bumping into something important, maybe."

"Or haunting them even though the big dance is coming up," said Gumluck.

"Or not buying enough ice cream," said Butterscotch.

"Can we stick with my example?" I asked. "About bumping? Mine was the best example."

I coughed and continued.

"Anyway," I said. "Forget that king. Forget those townspeople. You are better off without them."

Gumluck nodded a very little nod.

He said, "But . . . of course . . . if any of them *ask* for my help, then I should probably help them—"

"Oh, pooh!" I spat. "Did you not listen to a word I said?"

Gumluck shrank. Not by magic. I just mean he sat a little lower in his seat.

"Helping, helping!" I continued. "Always helping! Can no one ever help you?"

I hopped onto the windowsill and scowled.

"The king has no friends," I said. "And you haven't any, either."

Yes.

That is what I said.

Have you ever been trying to clean a dish, and you broke it instead? That was how I felt. I felt like I had broken something to pieces. Accidentally.

"I . . . need to work on my nest," I said.

And I turned and flew away before I broke anything else.

I left a woolly silence behind me. After a moment, Gumluck smiled at Butterscotch and said, "*You're* my friend."

"Ha ha!" said the ghost. "What an idea! Being friends with a house."

That night, Gumluck was visited by a fairy.

She fluttered in through a gap in the moonlit window. The air fizzed and shivered around her.

"Hello," whispered the wizard. The ghost snored. It was sleeping in Gumluck's hair.

"Forgive my friend," said Gumluck. "He is tired out from his long, exciting life. He was a warrior and had adventures."

No, said the fairy.

"No?"

He was ice cream, she said,

and he fell off his cone

and then melted and changed to a ghost, all alone.

Tears filled Gumluck's eyes. "That is the saddest story I have ever heard. Why did you tell it?"

TRUTH
FAIRY

Because that's what I do.

I tell things that are true.

"How do you know it is true?" asked Gumluck.

The fairy pointed to her shirt. The shirt said, TRUTH FAIRY.

"Oh!" said Gumluck. "You are the Truth Fairy."

The Truth Fairy visits at night, when you're trying to sleep. You can't really be sleeping, though. She won't come if you're sleeping.

The Truth Fairy sat atop a fat candlestick, so that the candle seemed to be lit with a sizzling light. Gumluck smiled carefully.

"Well. I am glad to meet you," he said.

Most people are glad when they meet me, you know,

but they're usually even more glad when I go.

"I am Gumluck," said the wizard. "People call me the Little Wizard Who Lives in the Big Hill."

That's what you thought,

but in truth? They do not.

Gumluck raised his eyebrows. "I think they do," he said.

The Truth Fairy didn't say anything.

Now Gumluck had a bad feeling in his stomach.

"Maybe Butterscotch lied about being a warrior," he admitted. "But the lie belonged to him. You gave it away."

The Truth Fairy still didn't say anything.

"Truth is good," added Gumluck, "but I think helping is better. The truth is only good when it helps. Did you . . . come here to help?"

Now the Truth Fairy drew closer and touched Gumluck's hand.

There are truths that are helpful, and hopeful as well.

But those kinds of truths . . . aren't the truths that I *tell.*

And then that fairy went and did it.

She told Gumluck everything.

She told Gumluck the truth about stars, and how far they are. To Gumluck it seemed far too far away.

She told him which came first, the chicken or the egg. When he heard it, Gumluck realized he liked the question better than the answer.

She told him how sausage is made. She told him things he did not wish to know about figs.

Of course, she told Gumluck that the people in town called him the Shrinking Wizard Who Lives Next to a Big Hole.

Which did not really matter—it was only a name. But then Gumluck remembered everything the townspeople had said about that Shrinking Wizard, and he understood that they had been saying those things about *him*.

Gumluck pulled the bedclothes over his nose. "What . . . what a bunch of lies you've told," he said. "*You* are no Truth Fairy. You are a . . . Lie Guy. You tell ridiculous lies."

He pulled the covers higher.

"I think it is time you left, *Lie Guy,*" said Gumluck.

That's true, and no lie,

said the fairy. *Goodbye.*

After she left, the room was silent but for the ghost's snoring. Silent, and very dark.

Then it brightened—someone was in the doorway.

(It was me. I was in the doorway.)

"Are you OK?" I asked. "I came back to . . . see how you were, and I saw something bright leave your window."

Gumluck sat up. "Tonight I had a visit from the Truth Fairy. Maybe."

Ah. So that's what it was. Something had shot like a comet across the yard as it left.

Totally wrecked my new nest, by the way.

"Oh," I said. "The Truth Fairy. I see."

Gumluck sniffed.

“And did this fairy talk about the people in town?” I asked him. “And in the castle?”

“Yes.”

“And did this fairy say anything about me?”

Gumluck tried to remember. “No,” he said. “She did not mention you.”

That was fine. I do not like to be talked about.

We sat quietly. For a while the quiet felt like a space between us. And after a little while longer the quiet felt like the space that held us together.

Finally, I hopped off the bed.

“Go to sleep,” I told him. “Tomorrow I will bake you a pie.”

Gumluck's Day Off

On Saturday Gumluck did not feel like doing anything at all. And that was a problem—because with nothing to do, he had nothing to do but think his thoughts. And he did not want to think about that fairy, or what the fairy had said.

So he tried not to do, and he tried not to think. He looked at the leaves and listened to the birds and felt an autumn breeze that smelled like pie. Apple pie—he could almost taste it. Maybe Butterscotch would like some with ice cream.

He had a feeling about Sunday. Sunday was going to be a busy day.

Gumluck the Greatest

Beyond the forest, in the center of the market square, the townspeople were holding the Harvest Dance. Everyone was there, even the king.

Past the market square, all the little houses sat empty. Past the houses was the king's tall, tall mountain. And at the very top of the king's tall, tall mountain—the castle creaked.

It shuddered, and creaked again.

It was heavy on one side. The side with the Treasure Room.

The king's Treasure Room had too much gold in it.

Down the mountain again, past the houses that were empty and the market that was full, far from the happy dancing, Gumluck the Wizard heard music.

This was the evening of the Harvest Dance, of course. He tapped his foot.

"Back when I was a great warrior I was also a great dancer!" said Butterscotch. He reeled around the room. "The greatest!"

Gumluck did not feel much like dancing anymore. It had been a long week. And an especially long Friday. "You should go," he said. "I may stay home this year, myself."

"But if you do not go, can they still name you the Harvest Hero?" asked the ghost. "Or will they have to name someone else? Like me."

Gumluck did not answer. He supposed the prince would probably just win again, anyway.

Far away in the market square a song ended and another began. But there was a different, louder sound as well, carried on the wind to the house in the hill. A *CRACK*.

A second later I flew to the window, wonder-struck.

Come quickly!

I said.

The townspeople need help.

In the market square, the band stopped playing. The eyes of all the townspeople turned upward.

Atop the king's mountain, another stone broke—CRACK—and the castle tipped . . . and fell.

“Heaven help us!” cried the people in the square.

“Have no fear!” Gumluck cried, running up out of breath. “It is me! The Little Wizard Who Lives in the Big Hill!” He thought of the Truth Fairy. He thought of shrinking and holes, then he took a breath. “I am here to help! Hello!”

Every man, woman, and child looked at Gumluck. Then at the downhill-crashing, swiftly tumbling castle. And then at Gumluck again.

"Ugh. Are there any *other* wizards here?!" shouted the prince.

"Only me!" said Gumluck. "Your favorite!"

The castle rolled like a giant die toward the empty houses.

"Mercy!" said the butcher. "Save our homes!"

"Yes," said Gumluck. "Here I go."

He raised his hands. He lowered his brows.

He had never tried to help so many people at once before.

"It . . . is a very big castle," he explained.

The castle crushed the houses. And kept rolling.

"Save US!" said the baker.

"Ah!" said Gumluck. "I know a good spell! If you believe in *me*, the Little Wizard Who Lives in the Big Hill, my spell will make you strong! Everyone who believes in me will become strong like a great warrior, and together we will *catch* the castle! Catch it and carry it away!"

"So . . . " said the butcher.

"Your spell will make us strong," said the baker.

"Yes!"

"Strong enough to catch a castle," said the candlestick maker.

"If you believe in me!" said Gumluck.

"But *only* if we believe in you," the prince sneered. "So if we don't, the spell won't work and we'll all be crushed."

"Exactly!" said Gumluck. "It's PERFECT!"

The people were quiet.

"Do you know any *other* spells?" shouted the king.

"Here I go," said Gumluck.

And as the castle charged toward them he cast his spell.

The spell fanned out over the people.

And the people . . . felt very much unchanged.

Then the massive castle rumbled and bounced one last bounce. The great shadow of it fell on them first, and then the rest of the castle followed.

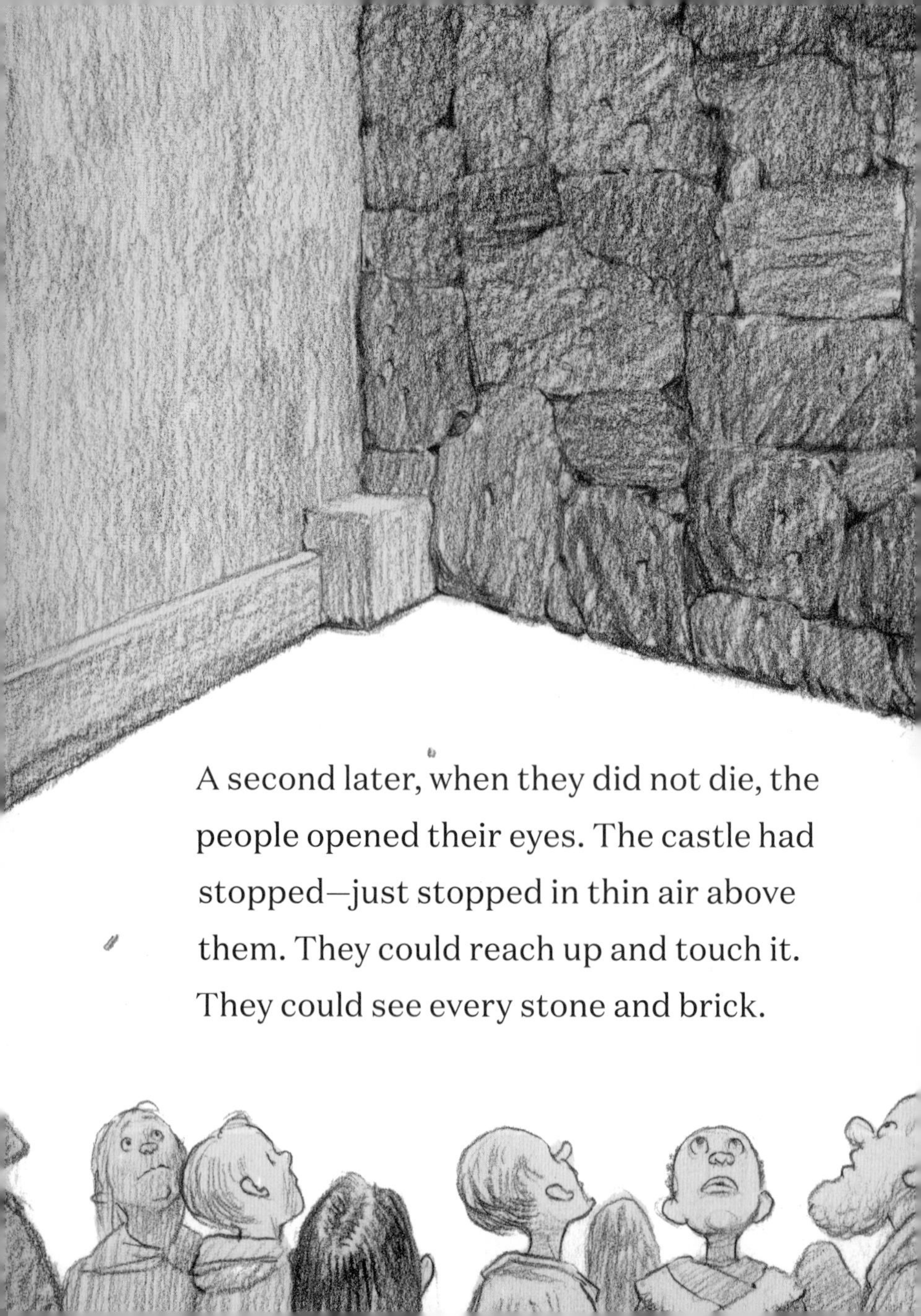

A second later, when they did not die, the people opened their eyes. The castle had stopped—just stopped in thin air above them. They could reach up and touch it. They could see every stone and brick.

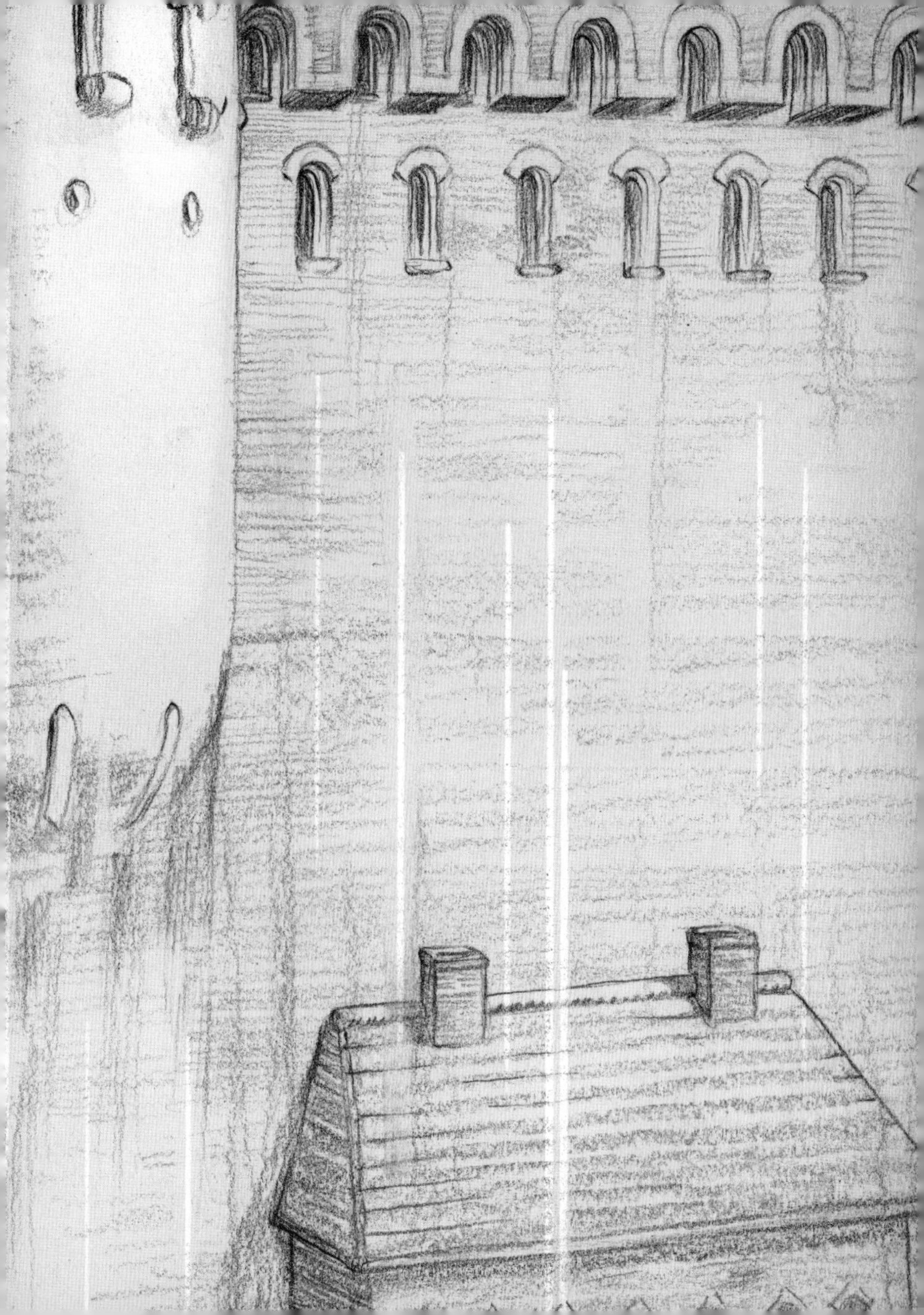

I had caught the castle in my claws and was madly flapping to keep us in flight.

"Little help?" I croaked.

And that was how I learned I believed in the wizard Gumluck. That was when I realized I loved him. What a way to find out.

Gumluck smiled up at me. The people looked at both of us in wonder. I believed in Gumluck, so finally, they did, too.

And once they believed in Gumluck they were made strong—just like he'd promised. Even Prince Whoop-de-doo.

In the end we all carried that castle together, and put it safely down by the mountain before the magic faded.

"I am sorry about your homes," Gumluck told them. "But! I know where there are some strong sticks and straw and bricks."

squeaked the king.

So the townspeople spent the evening building themselves new houses out of gold. Gumluck helped, of course. And when the houses were finished he called the stars down to light the way home.

The people walked silently through starlight. Silently they opened the doors of their starlit homes. They looked silently back at Gumluck without knowing what to say, and went to bed without saying a word.

"You're *welcome*!" I shouted.

Gumluck smiled and said, "I know how they feel."

It was late when we walked home. Leaves crunched beneath our feet. There was a soft moon behind a thin sheet of clouds, looking sleepy like people do when they're full.

I frowned at the flashy trash I was carrying. It was much too big and said HARVEST HERO on it in shiny letters. "What am I going to do with a crown?" I asked.

"It is yours," said Gumluck. "You may do whatever you wish."

I tossed it in the bushes.

"I am sorry they named me Harvest Hero instead of you," I told him.

"That is OK," said Gumluck. He sounded like he meant it. "I don't think I will worry so much about what the people name me, from now on."

Good.

"Do you know how we came to be friends?" I asked.

Gumluck scrunched up his face. It was something he did when he was thinking.

"Magic?" he asked. "It feels like magic."

I supposed it *had* been magic, in a way.

After all, it had been Gumluck's magic bucket that bumped—quite accidentally, I know—into my nest. Gumluck's magic that had caused the empty nest to fall to pieces on the ground.

I had been mad about that. I wasn't anymore. Gumluck's magic was what brought us together.

So I supposed I would tell him about it someday, but not today.

"Yes," I agreed. "Magic."

"I thought so," said Gumluck. He watched me and smiled. "You are in a fine mood."

"I *am*," I said. "There is something I've decided not to be mad about anymore, and that is a fine feeling."

Besides—I was about to make a *very* fine nest. I had taken some of the king's straw and sticks.

Gumluck had a funny look.

"Butterscotch says that when he was alive, he was a great warrior."

"Really? I was so sure he had been an ice cream scoop."

Gumluck jumped. "That is what the fairy said, too!"

"Well, I always feel cold when he is around."

"Oh, that is just a ghost thing," said Gumluck. "Ghosts make you cold."

"He also smells like vanilla."

"OK, true."

We'd walked a little farther when Gumluck suddenly stopped. So I stopped.

"I think Butterscotch was a great warrior," he said.

He scrunched up his face again, and this time I could see he really was thinking.

"A person should get to tell you who they are," he said. "And if they are living that life . . . then they need a family of friends who hear them tell it and say, *Yes, that's you, all right. We believe you.*"

He watched a leaf fall at his feet.

"I am Gumluck," he told the leaf. "And helping people is what *I* like about *myself.*"

The leaf was speechless.

(Not me, though.)

"Yes," I told Gumluck. "That's you all right. I believe you."

Gumluck nodded and kept walking, and I went along beside him.

If the Truth Fairy ever visits when *you* are trying to sleep, she might tell you there are no Happily Ever Afters. That's true—even happy lives have good days and bad.

Still, I wish the fairy had told Gumluck about that woman who came wanting a dress. Do you remember? She did get her dress in the end, sewn by tooth and beak and tiny claw. And would you guess her harvest dress looked more beautiful than any dress the kingdom had ever *seen*?

Well, it didn't. It looked weird. It was made by mice and birds.

It looked so weird and made the woman so unhappy she ran crying into the street and was nearly run down by a speeding wagon—a wagon that was stopped just in time by a man with magically large muscles. They are getting married in the spring.

That is a pretty happy ending.

And that fussy prince? He tripped and fell into a pile of horse droppings.

That's a happy ending, too, if you ask me.

Gumluck Ever After

We got home so late that we had walked out of Sunday and straight into Monday.

"It is Monday!" said Gumluck the Wizard.

"Again," I said. The sun was just squinting over the hill.

"Where has the week gone," said Gumluck. He scratched his head. "I hope we do not have any visitors from town—I'm bushed."

He frowned at his house.

"Helvetica, is that how big my hill is?" he asked. "That's too big."

"Oh, foo," I laughed. "You darling old noodle-head."

ADAM REX is the author and illustrator of many beloved books, including the *New York Times* bestseller *Frankenstein Makes a Sandwich*. He has illustrated the work of many authors, including Jon Scieszka, Mac Barnett, Jeff Kinney, Kate DiCamillo, Eoin Colfer, Christopher Paul Curtis, Paul Feig, and Neil Gaiman. He lives in Tucson, Arizona. See more about him at www.adamrex.com.